Max Rhymes™
A Children's Series

Max & Molly
Learn Their Manners

Teaching core values, creating higher self-esteem and
increasing reading retention, all through the power of rhymes.

Todd & Jackie Courtney

Max & Molly Learn Their Manners
Max Rhymes™

Illustration and Copyright © 2018 by Inspired Imaginations, LLC

ISBN: 978-1-945200-24-3

Library of Congress Control Number: 2017919833

Published by:
Inspired Imaginations, LLC

Websites

MaxRhymes.com   MaxRhymesClub.com   MaxRhymesFoundation.org

Words to Know
A Pre-Reading Activity

ACCIDENTAL   happening by chance, or unexpectedly, or unintentionally.

ADDRESS   the place where a person or organization can be found or communicated with.

EXCUSED   to forgive someone for making a mistake; doing something wrong.

INTERRUPT   to ask a question or say things while another person is speaking; to do or say something that causes someone to stop speaking.

MANNERS   somewhat formal; the way that something is done or happens.

NAPKIN   a small piece of cloth or paper used during a meal to clean your lips and fingers and to protect your clothes.

NEIGHBOR   a person who lives next to you or near another person.

POLITENESS   having or showing good manners or respect for other people.

When you meet someone new
or haven't seen for a while,
always shake their hand
while giving them a smile.

When I address someone older,
like a neighbor or family friend,
I begin with Mr. & Mrs.
and put their last name at the end.

If a burp comes out
in an accidental way,
it's best to say excuse me
and then continue to play.

You should always chew
with your mouth being closed.
Make sure you don't talk,
and breathe through your nose.

When mommy is on the phone
talking to a friend,
it's not polite to interrupt her
until she hangs up at the end.

Cover your mouth
when you cough and sneeze.
Blow your nose
with a tissue, please.

When you come into the house
and food is ready to eat,
be sure to wash your hands first
before you take your seat.

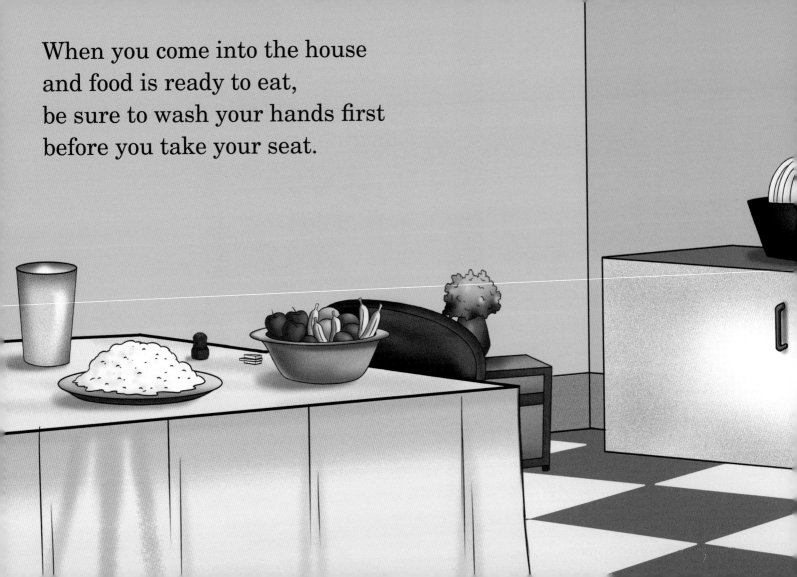

Napkins on your lap
and elbows off the table.
Feet on the floor
for everyone who is able.

Before I leave the table,
I ask to be excused.
It's a reminder of politeness
and politeness should always be used.

Mama

Papa

Max

Molly

Rosie

Kenny

Stella

Ricky

Did you find Max's hidden books?

SYNOPSIS

Max & Molly Learn Their Manners is a collection of rhymes that focus on inspiring children to use manners such as Mr.& Mrs., "please" and "thank you," shaking hands, common courtesy and more. Each rhyme is affirming a belief that will develop a sense of ownership from their actions, accountability, and an awareness of others.

THEME

Max & Molly Learn Their Manners is ideal for teaching children social skills to last a life time. Learning how to greet people, say "please" & "thank you" at the appropriate times, being kind, sharing, not interrupting, table manners and so much more. Children may be born with a number of innate abilities, but behaving with polite manners is not one of them. Manners, once learned, will stick with repetition.

TEACHER IDEAS

Greeting People:
Review with the students what is happening in the picture with Stella and Papa.

Reread the rhyme:

"When you meet someone new or haven't seen for a while, always shake their hand while giving them a smile."

Have students share how they would greet someone walking into the classroom, meeting a parent, friend, neighbor or how they should introduce themselves. Role play just like Papa and Stella do in the picture.

Stella: "Hi, I'm Stella. It's nice to meet you."
Papa: "It's nice to meet you too, Stella."

"Please" & "Thank You":

Review with the students what is happening with Max & Molly at the park with their friends.

Reread the rhyme:

"The most important words that should be in your head are "please" and "thank you" and they should always be said."

Have students draw or paint pictures of activities where they should say "please" and "thank you" like Max and his friends did at the park.

Table Etiquette:

Review with your students the importance of good table manners when eating at school, a friend's house, a restaurant or at home.

Reread the rhyme:

"Napkins on your lap and elbows off the table. Feet on the floor for everyone who is able."

Ask the children to look at the picture and discuss what is happening.

Point out that everyone's napkins are on their laps and feet are on the floor for those who are able. Who's feet are on the floor?

Max Rhymes™ Books

A Children's Series

Be Responsible Like Max

Get Inspired with Max

Giving Thanks with Max

Max Gives Thanks to God

Max & Molly Learn Their Manners

Daydream with Max & Molly

The Science Behind Our Rhymes

Did you know questions:

- Did you know that 95% of our behavioral patterns are established by the age of 7?
- Did you know that babies recognize words, sounds and feelings while in the womb?
- Did you know that due to brain waves changes at such early stages in life, science tells us we should begin teaching our babies in utero?
- Did you know that the science of epigenetics has proven that our thoughts can modify our gene expression?
- Did you know that only 1 out of 10 adults ever change their behavioral patterns for the better, which confirms what science is telling us? That is, we should be teaching our infants and toddlers the positive virtues we want them to have in life prior to age 7.

Let's talk about brain waves!

A baby is born in a delta brain wave frequency. This is the lowest frequency and is the reason why their brains are like little sponges. Around age 2, the brain changes into a theta frequency which is still a low frequency, but higher than delta. This just means the brain will be a little less spongy than the delta frequency. However, around age 7, we move into an alpha frequency, which is a much higher frequency, and makes us less susceptible to learn so easily. In essence, it's kind of like being on auto pilot from age 7. Sounds scary, doesn't it? Around age 12 we move into a beta frequency, which is even higher, and the reason so many teenagers have a tough time learning things such as foreign languages. So, why is this important to know? Because it provides the science to back up why it's imperative to teach our infants and toddlers positive virtues prior to them reaching the age of 7.

What makes Max Rhymes different?

Due to early brainwave changes, science has proven the learning stage between ages 0–7 is one of the most important of our lives. Max Rhymes takes advantage of this learning period by teaching core values, creating a positive belief system, increasing reading retention and creating higher self-esteem, all through the power of rhymes.

Want to learn about epigenetics?

Keep reading!

Epigenetics:

the study of changes in organisms caused by modification of gene expression rather than alteration of the genetic code itself.

What does that mean to you as a parent?

It means you have a lot more influence on your child than we ever knew. Did you know that you have an impact on your child's IQ? Did you know that you have an impact on your child even before conception? Most of us didn't and still don't know this. However, research is revealing what others, such as aboriginal cultures, have known for 1000 years and it's why those cultures go through a ceremony to purify their minds and bodies.

Research is showing that parents, by default, act as genetic engineers months before conception. During the final stages of egg and sperm maturation, a process called genomic imprinting adjusts the activity of specific groups of genes that will shape the characteristics of the child yet to be conceived. (The Biology of Belief, Bruce Lipton; Surani 2001; Reik and Walter 2001) What that means is your stress levels, be it financial, relationship, family, friends, work, etc. and likewise your level of happiness and peacefulness, all play a role in the development of your child even before conception.

Now, on top of that, add the fact that **95% of the programming to the subconscious mind is done by the age of 7**. That means all the things your child has heard via conversations, TV or radio, is all getting programmed in the mind. It's this programming that plays a huge role in the child's future based on the "truths" and "beliefs" the child has been programmed with. Unfortunately, most of us have been programmed with limitations, which has prevented us from creating the life we deserve.

Endorsed By

"Language acquisition plays a fundamental role in exercising an infant's brain and shaping its intelligence. Research reveals that interactive social experiences with parents, through conversation and reading, provides a gateway to enhancing a child's linguistic, cognitive, and emotional development.

The social programming a child receives before age seven is the primary determinant of its health and fate as an adult. I encourage parents, grandparents and extended family members to review the new series of Max Rhymes by Todd and Jackie Courtney. Their compilations of beautifully illustrated, consciousness-enhancing messages are designed to elicit a child's intelligence, integrity, and respect for others and our planet. Max Rhymes is a powerful tool to help children reach their full potential … a benefit for all of humanity, since a child's behavior will ultimately influence the evolution of us all."

–Bruce H. Lipton, Ph.D.
Cell biologist, Specialist in Epigenetics, and
best-selling author of *The Biology of Belief*

About the Authors

Jacqueline "Jackie" Courtney, was born and raised in San Jose, CA. and has spent most of her life as an elementary school teacher in the grades of kindergarten through 3rd. With her talents as a teacher and private tutor, specializing in the area of reading, it was a natural for Jackie to follow her passion in the creation of children's books.

Todd J. Courtney was raised in San Jose, CA for most of his life. He has spent the past 29 years as a business owner and during the last 5 years, he was teaching what Wallace D. Wattles calls "thinking stuff" to business groups. As a devoted study on behavioral science and thought-provoking philosophy, he authored, *Thinking In One Direction,* which targets teens and young adults. To expand on the books philosophy, he created www.TeensCanDream.org; a site dedicated to help teens during those tumultuous years. He then created an animation video for children with leukemia called, *Just Imagine If…You were leukemia free!* www.JustImagineIf.org. Thereafter, he co-authored, with his wife Jackie, *Max Rhymes,* a children's book series with the purpose of bringing core values back into the mainstream. He is the founder of the Max Rhymes Foundation.